old
mrs. mopiter

by James Young

PRICE STERN SLOAN
Los Angeles

Library of Congress Cataloging-in-Publication Data

Young, James, 1956-
    Old Mrs. Mopiter / by James Young.
        p.   cm.
    Summary: A zany old lady and her spirited dog share a hilarious
and eventful day.
    ISBN 0-8431-2359-1   : $6.95
    [1. Dogs—Fiction.   2.Stories in rhyme.]   I. Title.
PZ8.3.Y78701   1989   88-8537
[E]—dc19   CIP
                                                AC

Old Mrs. Mopiter,
Early one morning,
Crept downstairs
Without any warning.
And caught ol' Bo
At the kitchen table
Drinking coffee
And eating a bagel.

Old Mrs. Mopiter,
In her pajamas,
Sat in a rocking chair
Eating bananas.
Bo walked up
And he wanted a bite,
So she gave him the peels
And they tasted just right.

Old Mrs. Mopiter,
Wouldn't you know?
Had a garden
That wouldn't grow.
Had a garden
That wouldn't sprout.
The seeds went in
But nothing came out.
When all at once
It began to rain
And up popped her flowers,
Her fruits, her grain.

Old Mrs. Mopiter out in her garden,
Stepped on a snake and begged its pardon.

"Thath alright, my dear Mithes Mopither.
I alwayth wanted a tail that wath floppier."

Old Mrs. Mopiter
Chasing a rabbit,
Jumped in the air
And tried to grab it.
But quick as she was,
The rabbit was quicker,
The rabbit was faster,
The rabbit was slicker.
" You'll never catch me,
My dear Mrs. Mopiter!"
And away he ran—
Hippity hoppiter.

Old Mrs. Mopiter,
Climbing a tree,
Ran into
A big bumblebee.
She said "Boo!"
The bee said, "Buzz?"
And off it flew,
Just because.

Old Mrs. Mopiter,
Milking a cow,
Didn't know why,
Didn't know how.
Didn't know one end
From the udder,
So got no milk,
No cream, no butter.

Old Mrs. Mopiter,
Washing her socks,
Turned around
And saw a fox.
"Old Mrs. Mopiter,
Please," he said,
"I must have a pair
To wear on my head!"

Old Mrs. Mopiter
Mopping the floor,
When suddenly Bo
Ran in the door
Chasing a cat
That was chasing a mouse
That was chasing a fly
All over the house.
She dropped her mop
And grabbed a broom
And chased every one of them
Out of the room.

Old Mrs. Mopiter
Made a cake,
Put it in
The oven to bake,
Turned it up
To a hundred and one
And took it out when
It was done.

Old Mrs. Mopiter
Couldn't remember
If she had been born
In July or December,
In August or April,
In May or November.
"Well," Mrs. Mopiter
Said with a grin,
"As long as I was,
I don't care when."

Old Mrs. Mopiter thought she'd go fishing,
But the fish wouldn't bite,
So she sat there a-wishing.
She pulled up her line to get a good look—
A frog was stealing the worms off her hook!
"Get him, Bo!" yelled Old Mrs. Mopiter.

The dog jumped in
And the frog jumped up at her.

Old Mrs. Mopiter
Went for a ride,
But right or left she
Couldn't decide.
Left or right?
Around? Ahead?
So she went back home
And got into bed.

Old Mrs. Mopiter
In a heap.
Her toes stick out
From under the sheet.
She counts her toes
Instead of sheep,
And that's the way
She goes to sleep.
Bo snores peacefully
On top of her.
Now say good night
To Old Mrs. Mopiter.